ISBN: 978-1-950817-01-6 (Paperback)
ISBN: 978-1-950817-00-9 (Hardcover)
ISBN: 978-1-950817-02-3 (E-book)
ISBN: 978-1-950817-05-4 (Audiobook)

Any references to historical events, real people, or real places, are used fictitiously.
Names, characters, and places are products of the author's imagination.

Front cover image by Milena Matić.

Printed by Power Corner Press, in the United States of America

First printing edition 2019.

Power Corner Press
1360 University Ave W Ste #351
Saint Paul, MN, 55104

www.powercornerpress.com

Baby
Daisy

For Kay Kay,
Even though your screams and cries hurt my ears,
I still think you're cute.
💕kisses💕

Each morning when I wake up,
I head straight to the crib.

Mom puts on Kay Kay's onesie;
I put on her matching bib.

At the breakfast table,
between bites of syrupy toast,

I feed Kay Kay banana oatmeal;
she loves sweets the most!

When I must go off to school,
Kay Kay is sometimes sad.

I tell her I will be back soon
and after me comes Dad.

I have a bright surprise for Kay Kay
when I get home later.

A drawing of us that Mommy hangs
high on the refrigerator.

Uh oh, Kay Kay has lost her pacifier,
once again!

Me–Ma searches the kitchen;
Grandad scours the den.

I get on my hands and knees
and check every small space.

I find it, wash away the germs
and put it back in place.

Kay Kay needs a diaper change;
I squeeze onto my nose.

She smells but she's a baby
and can't help it I suppose.

I hand Mommy a fresh diaper
for Kay Kay to wear...

...But Kay Kay sends a stream of water up into the air!

It's time to see the doctor;
Kay Kay needs her shots.

From the last time that we went,
I know it hurts a lot.

When Kay Kay comes out crying,
I sing a silly song.

I wipe away her tears
and she's better before long.

Mom sits on a park bench
and takes care of our things.

I hold Kay Kay's hand
and walk her slowly to the swings.

Afterwards, when we get home, it's time for us to bake.
Delicious, crunchy cookies are our favorite treats to make.

One night, Kay Kay is fussy;
her temperature is high.

Mom gives her baby medicine
and rocks her with a sigh.

I read the story she likes best as she cuddles close to me.
It's the one about a mermaid who lives beneath the sea.

Kay Kay and I like to watch
cartoons on the couch together.

It's something that we do
especially in not-so-good weather.

Mommy and Daddy like to join us;
We're happy as can be!

Even Prince, the family dog,
snuggles up with his blankie.

I love playtime in my bedroom,
with lots of dollhouse fun.

Kay Kay always comes
and makes a mess before I'm done.

I play in the upstairs
while Kay Kay plays down below.

She keeps eating my Barbie's nose,
even when I say no!

Kay Kay is my favorite—yes—even with tearful eyes.
That just means I must whip up another fun surprise.

Kay Kay is the best baby sister;
She loves my silly songs.

She claps her hands, kicks her feet,
and tries to sing along.

When it's time to go to bed,
Kay Kay and I get in the tub.

I take a soapy washcloth;
I scrub and scrub and scrub.

Kay Kay squeals and splashes;
there's water everywhere!

This is just another
of the joyful times we share.

I love my baby sister
and wouldn't trade her for another.

It's great to have a sister
and pretend that I'm a mother.

I'll teach my little Kay Kay
every single thing I know.

I'll stay a proud big sister
and watch her as she grows.

Made in the USA
Monee, IL
05 November 2020